Josh
10/1/94

The Doggonest
Puppy Love

Dear Kevin,

Dare to Love!

Richard Stack

The Doggonest Puppy Love

by
Richard Lynn Stack

Illustrations by Chet Phillips

The Doggonest Puppy Love

by Richard Lynn Stack

Illustrations by Chet Phillips

Other books by Richard Stack

The Doggonest Christmas
Illustrations by Charles W. Stack

The Doggonest Vacation
Illustrations by Sheri Mowrer

Printed in USA by Taylor Publishing Company, Dallas.

Distributed by:

Windmill Press
7609 Beaver Road
Glen Burnie, MD 21060

ISBN 0-9628262-1-9

Dedicated to Marla June Stack,
who loves Josh, The Wonder Dog
almost as much as the author.

It was February in the little town of Bobsled, and everyone had a sweetheart — except for Josh. Valentine's Day was drawing near, and the little dog was feeling very lonely.

All of Josh's friends had sweethearts. Bobo was spending a lot of time over at Fluffy's house. Blackie liked to make dreamy eyes at Princess. And Willie was always walking with Bootsie over at Snowshoe Point.

Even Miss Elly had a sweetheart, although she never found out who he was. One afternoon, the town florist delivered a box of beautiful red roses to her house. Josh watched as his owner rummaged through the box, and found a little card tucked inside. Written on the card was a poem.

Miss Elly asked who had sent the flowers. The florist told her that they were from a secret admirer.

"Wow, Oh Bow Wow!" yapped Josh, as Miss Elly blushed delicately.

Although Josh was happy for everyone else, he longed for a sweetheart to call his own. His friends were more than willing to give their advice.

"Maybe you should go out with Judy," suggested Willie. "When I say your names together, it sounds good."

"Josh and Judy . . . Josh and Judy," Willie said over and over.

"I guess it does," answered Josh, "but that's not how I'd choose a valentine."

"Well then, little Bonnie would be perfect for you," offered Fido. "Both of you are small, and you look good standing side by side." The friends nodded in agreement.

"Thanks, guys" replied Josh, "but there *must* be a better way to find someone who's right for me."

The gray sky of winter made Josh feel even lonelier. He decided to talk with Phil, a wise old groundhog who lived on the other side of Bobsled. Josh scooted over to Phil's burrow, which was nestled deep in a mound of dirt.

A few days earlier, the burrow had been bustling with activity. Everyone was there on Groundhog's Day to find out when Old Man Winter would be leaving. But today, Phil's home was peaceful and quiet.

Josh called down into the burrow. In a moment, Phil's head popped out.

"Hi, little buddy," said Phil cheerily. "Why the glum face?"

Before he realized what he was saying, Josh blurted out something he had not told his other friends.

"I know who I want my sweetheart to be," the little dog confessed. "But I'm afraid my friends will think I'm being silly."

Josh told Phil that on a brisk October day, he and Miss Elly had taken the morning ferry over to Iceland. They had gone there hoping to see the great whales, which were migrating south for the winter. This was the perfect place to watch them.

Standing beneath a dome of the bluest sky they had ever seen, Josh and Miss Elly waited with anticipation. As they watched, a gigantic humpback whale surfaced from the depths of the sea.

° FEBR

S	M	T
	1	2

"Wow, Oh Bow Wow!" Josh had shouted excitedly, as the humpback smacked its tail down against the ocean.

"Ker-pow!" went the huge tail. "Ker-pow! Ker-pow!"

"That looks like fun!" Josh had yapped, as he scooted over to a puddle of water. Then he had spun around, and slapped his tail down with all his might.

"Ka-pop!" went his little tail. "Ka-pop! Ka-pop!"

Miss Elly had looked on approvingly. She knew how important it was that Josh try things for himself. But the little dog had felt embarrassed. Compared with the efforts of the whale, he saw his own as puny and weak.

Josh had looked around, hoping that no one else was watching him. He had noticed a red and white dog, sitting near a crowd of people. She was looking right at him, and smiling from ear to ear. To Josh, she was the most beautiful creature he had ever seen.

As the crowd started walking down the shoreline, the red and white dog had turned and smiled again.

"She probably saw me 'playing whale' and thinks I'm dumb!" Josh had muttered to himself. Miss Elly could tell what her little dog was thinking.

"She doesn't think you're dumb," said Miss Elly. "She likes you, Josh!"

Miss Elly had told Josh that some people in the crowd were leaders of great countries. They had come to Iceland for a meeting called a "summit."

"That dog lives in a big white house," said Miss Elly, "with some remarkable people. One of them is named Lady Barbara. The other is the most important person in the world. He is called 'Mr. President.' "

"And the dog who has captured your heart is named Millie."

When Josh finished telling his story, Phil let a long whistle escape between his big front teeth.

"Gosh, little buddy, I wish I could help you," said Phil. "But you see, when it comes to sweethearts — and the weather, I'm scared of my own shadow. Gotta go now!"

With that, Phil waved good-bye and disappeared into his burrow. Josh was left sitting by himself, and feeling lonelier than ever.

When Josh returned home, Miss Elly could see that he was unhappy. She sat down and lifted her little dog onto her lap.

"Josh," she said gently, "you shouldn't be worried that you don't have a girlfriend yet. Young dogs are just like young people. You want to fit in, and be like your friends. But you mustn't do something that isn't right for you, just to be one of the crowd."

"You've decided that Millie is the girl of your dreams," continued Miss Elly. "But there is only one way to know for sure. Let's go to Washington, D.C., and see if you can meet her."

"Wow, Oh Bow Wow!" shouted the little dog, as he showered Miss Elly with lots of big kisses. "I'm going to tell my friends!"

"You can't be serious," said Brownie, when Josh admitted his feelings for Millie.

"Why would she want to be *your* girlfriend?" Bowser chimed in. "She's the most famous dog in the world!" The other friends laughed loudly.

Josh smiled at the other dogs, and walked away with his head held high. He had learned to pay no attention when the friends acted this way. Besides, he had to get ready to travel!

Several days later, Miss Elly and Josh arrived in Washington. The little dog could hardly believe that he was there. Everywhere he looked was something he had only seen in pictures. The Capitol! The Washington Monument! The Lincoln Memorial!

After they had checked into their motel, Josh and Miss Elly walked up Pennsylvania Avenue. The little dog could not feel his feet under him, for this was Millie's street.

When they reached the White House, they saw a long line of people waiting to go inside. Josh was tingling all over as he and Miss Elly went to the back of the line.

"Wow, Oh Bow Wow!" Josh yapped. "We're finally here!"

Slowly, they moved closer to the gate. But as they reached the front of the line, a policeman walked over to them.

"I'm sorry," the policeman said to Miss Elly, "but dogs are not allowed into the White House."

"How can that be?" Josh wondered to himself. "Millie *lives* in the White House!"

"Sometimes there are rules which don't seem fair," said Miss Elly as she stepped out of line. "Let's go, Josh."

Miss Elly smiled down at her little dog. Josh did not understand what was happening, but gave up his place also.

Miss Elly and Josh walked down the street, beside a tall fence which encircled the White House lawn. The little dog was devastated, his head hanging down so low that it almost scraped the sidewalk.

Josh became aware of something moving on the other side of the fence. He looked up and found himself nose-to-nose with Millie.

Josh stared into the eyes of his beautiful dream-girl. He tried to speak but could not make his voice work. Then Millie pressed her cold nose against his.

"Wow, Oh Bow Wow!" Josh whispered to himself. "She remembers me!"

Josh heard someone calling Millie's name. He looked up, and saw Lady Barbara walking toward them. Miss Elly introduced herself and Josh to Lady Barbara, and soon was explaining why they had come to Washington. Lady Barbara laughed when Miss Elly related what had just happened at the gate. She asked if they would still like to see the White House. Miss Elly replied that they would be thrilled.

Miss Elly and Josh walked back to the entrance, expecting to wait again in the long line. But as they approached the gate, the policeman was waiting for them. He looked puzzled.

"I've been instructed to bring you right into the White House," the policeman said to Miss Elly. "And of course, your little dog may go in, too," he added sheepishly.

Miss Elly and Josh were ushered into the White House. Inside, they were met by Lady Barbara and Millie, who greeted them warmly. Josh decided that Lady Barbara looked a lot like Miss Elly. Both of them had white hair and an engaging smile.

The White House was simply beautiful. Magnificent paintings graced the walls, and the rooms were decorated with the most elegant furniture. Josh was worried that he might break something, and was afraid to move. Lady Barbara knew a lot about dogs, and could tell what he was thinking.

"Relax, Josh," she said in a reassuring voice. "My grandchildren play in here all the time. You can't hurt anything — as long as you watch out for that tail of yours."

Josh looked back. His tail was wagging back and forth faster than a high-speed windshield wiper! Miss Elly and Lady Barbara laughed. Millie was laughing, too.

After they had toured the White House, Miss Elly and Lady Barbara sat in a cozy parlor, swapping their favorite recipes and bragging about their dogs. They discovered that they liked many of the same things.

Millie and Josh sat nearby, talking and learning about each other.

"I was hoping that you'd remember me," Josh admitted to Millie.

"How could I forget you?" she answered. "The last time I saw you, you were trying to imitate a big whale!"

"You saw me doing that?" asked Josh. "I was worried that someone might think I was acting dumb."

"That's what I liked about you," said Millie. "You weren't afraid to try something, just because of what someone else might think!"

"Wow, Oh Bow Wow!" said Josh. "That's what Miss Elly likes about me, too!"

"Come on, Josh," said Millie, as she took off running down the hall. Josh ran after her, and caught up just as Millie nudged open a door. Josh followed her into a room which was shaped like a big egg.

"This is the Oval Office," said Millie. "This is where my dad works."

All of a sudden Millie bounded across the room and jumped up onto a fancy desk. Josh jumped up right behind her.

"Wow, Oh Bow Wow!" shouted Millie.

"Oh, my gosh!" gulped Josh, as he skidded to a stop. Sitting behind the desk was the most important person in the world.

"Well, Millie," chuckled Mr. President, "who's your handsome little boyfriend?" Josh could feel his face turning as red as Millie's long ears.

Lovingly, Mr. President wrapped his arms around Millie and Josh, hugging them tightly. Millie and Josh were squirming so much that without warning, Mr. President's chair tipped over with a loud crash. The three of them went sprawling onto the thick carpet which covered the floor.

At once, the door to the Oval Office flew open, and in rushed some men in uniforms. They looked worried.

"I'm all right, gentlemen," laughed Mr. President, making no effort to get up. The men breathed a big sigh of relief as they left the room.

Mr. President lay on the floor, laughing loudly as Josh and Millie hopped over and around him. They were having so much fun that none of them noticed Lady Barbara and Miss Elly walk in.

"I should have known I'd find you in here," Lady Barbara said to Millie. "You know better than to bother your dad when he's working."

"Shucks, they aren't bothering me," said Mr. President. "I can't remember the last time I had this much fun! I hope Millie's little friend will be staying around for a while. He's good company for her."

"And for you, too," observed Lady Barbara. "Well, I'd like you to meet Miss Elly. You've already met Josh. I've invited them to stay with us while they're here in Washington."

"Terrific," said Mr. President, as he stood up to shake Miss Elly's outstretched hand. "We're having a State dinner on Saturday for the Queen of Irabia. I'd love for you to be our guest at the dinner."

"And Josh can be Millie's date," added Lady Barbara. "After all, Saturday is Valentine's Day."

"Wow, Oh Bow Wow!" said Josh and Millie, as their faces lit up with excitement.

Miss Elly and Josh were given the honor of staying in the Lincoln Bedroom. Josh jumped up onto the bed, to see where he would be sleeping.

"That bed is over eight feet long," Miss Elly told him. "A lady named Mary Lincoln bought it, over a hundred years ago, when her husband was 'Mr. President.' His name was Abraham, and he was a very tall man. He probably didn't sleep in that bed, but other 'Mr. Presidents' did."

"Wow, Oh Bow Wow!" exclaimed Josh, as he wondered how many "Mr. Presidents" there had been.

Everyone at the White House was looking forward to the Queen's visit. She was a kind and gentle leader, who worked very hard for the people of Irabia.

Some people in Irabia were not kind, however, and always wanted their own way. When they could not have their way, they did things which hurt other people. The Queen and Mr. President were hoping to find a way to solve Irabia's problems.

On Saturday morning, Josh and Millie watched excitedly as a limousine drove up to the White House. It was shiny and all black, and had Irabian flags fluttering on the front fenders. When the Queen stepped out, Josh was surprised that she was so young and beautiful.

Josh and Millie tagged along as Lady Barbara showed the Queen to the Rose Guest Room. In her honor, it had been re-named the Queen's Bedroom. Josh was thrilled that the Queen would be staying just across the hall from him.

"So this is your famous dog," laughed the Queen as she scooped Millie up in her arms.

"And this is her little boyfriend," said Lady Barbara, as she picked up Josh.

Later that day, everyone started dressing for the big dinner. Miss Elly put on a dress that she had bought especially for the occasion. Josh watched as she pinned on a flower which Mr. President had sent to the room. Josh wondered whether Mr. President was Miss Elly's secret admirer.

"The very idea!" Miss Elly chuckled.

When Josh and Miss Elly came downstairs, they found the White House swarming with news reporters. People all over the world were heartened by the Queen's visit, and anxious to hear about it.

When the Queen had been introduced to the dinner guests, everyone went into the State Dining Room. Millie and Josh sat at a little table, which had been set especially for them.

"I wonder what we're having for dinner?" Josh asked his pretty date.

"I don't know for sure," laughed Millie, "but if I know my dad, it won't be broccoli. Dad *hates* broccoli!"

As Josh and Millie were talking, the Queen walked over to their table. Everyone watched as she knelt down beside Millie.

"My dog could not come with me on this trip," said the Queen. "So she sent you some of her own special treats. I hope you like them."

The Queen reached out her hand, which held a delicious-looking dog cookie. As Millie gobbled down the treat, a peculiar look came over her face.

"I don't feel well," whispered Millie as she closed her eyes.

With that, she collapsed into the arms of the Queen. Lady Barbara and Mr. President rushed over to see what had happened. In no time at all, a doctor was there also.

"I'm not sure," said the doctor, "but I think she's been poisoned!"

"Poisoned?" cried Lady Barbara. "How can that be?"

"I think I know," said the Queen as her eyes welled up with tears. "I fed her one of these," she added as she showed them the treats.

"Someone from my country must have put poison in the cookies. They were trying to harm my dog, but hurt Millie instead."

As Lady Barbara carried Millie up to bed, Miss Elly tried to calm Josh. He could not understand how someone could do such a terrible thing.

"Josh, I've taught you that it's important for each of us to follow our dreams. But that doesn't allow us to hurt others, just to make our own dreams come true. Whoever did this was selfish and cruel."

A little while later, Lady Barbara walked back into the room. She was shaking her head, and tears were streaming down her cheeks.

"The doctor says that there is no cure for the poison," said Lady Barbara. "He says that without one, Millie will surely die."

"My heavens," said Miss Elly, as she jumped up with a start. "I know a cure. I learned it from my mother, when I was a little girl."

Miss Elly rushed down to the White House kitchen, with Josh and Lady Barbara close behind her. They watched as Miss Elly took some things from the pantry, and cooked them into a strange-smelling medicine. When it was ready, she handed it to Lady Barbara.

"Please ask the doctor to feed this to your dog," said Miss Elly. "And ask everyone to pray for her. We'll need all the prayers we can get."

The news that Millie might die spread quickly around the world. And everywhere the story was reported, a little dog named Josh was shown sitting beside Millie's bed. His eyes were tightly closed, and his head was bowed in prayer. It was a picture that touched every heart.

Back in the little town of Bobsled, pictures of Josh and Millie flashed across television screens in every home.

"I don't believe my eyes," said Bowser. "Josh met Millie — just as he said he would!"

"And now he needs our help," said Blackie. The rest of the friends agreed and quietly bowed their heads.

All over the world, people and dogs began praying for Millie. They prayed in churches, in their homes, and even on street corners.

And little by little, Millie began to get well.

"Wow, Oh Bow Wow!" were the first words Millie heard when she finally woke up. They were whispered by a little dog named Josh, who had sat day and night praying by Millie's bedside.

"The doctor says that Millie will be as good as new," announced Lady Barbara. "We owe it all to Miss Elly and her medicine."

"There is something I must tell you," said Miss Elly. "Many years ago, my mother taught me that when things seem hopeless, prayers may be our only answer. So I found a way to make everyone want to pray for Millie. You see, there was nothing in my medicine to help her. It was everyone's prayers that saved your beautiful dog."

Soon, Millie was romping around the White House, and playing with Josh again. Somehow, the world seemed a better place now. Even the people of Irabia were trying to solve their problems peacefully. They had learned that hurting others was not the way to make their dreams come true.

To show his gratitude, Mr. President awarded Miss Elly and Josh the Medal of Freedom, the highest honor he could bestow upon them.

"You have taught us all a valuable lesson," declared Mr. President. "You are two of the thousand points of light I have been hoping for. Lady Barbara and I thank you from the bottom of our hearts."

Finally, it was time for Miss Elly and Josh to say good-bye. Mr. President's own special airplane, Air Force One, was waiting to take them home.

When Air Force One landed at Bobsled Airport, the whole town turned out to greet Josh and Miss Elly.

"Wow, Oh Bow Wow!" Josh yapped when he saw his friends waving and cheering. The friends were anxious to hear about his adventure, which Josh delighted in telling. But as often as he recounted his story, the friends begged to hear it "just one more time."

One day, Josh learned that Millie had fallen in love with a dog named Tug. Millie became the proud mother of six beautiful puppies. Josh was happy that Millie had found a sweetheart who was right for her. And he was sure that he would someday find a girl who was just right for him. In the meantime, he would be content, knowing that Miss Elly loved him very much.

Josh's First Love

But for the little while that Josh had known
Millie, it was the doggonest puppy love ever.